Were You a Wild Duck Where Would You Go?

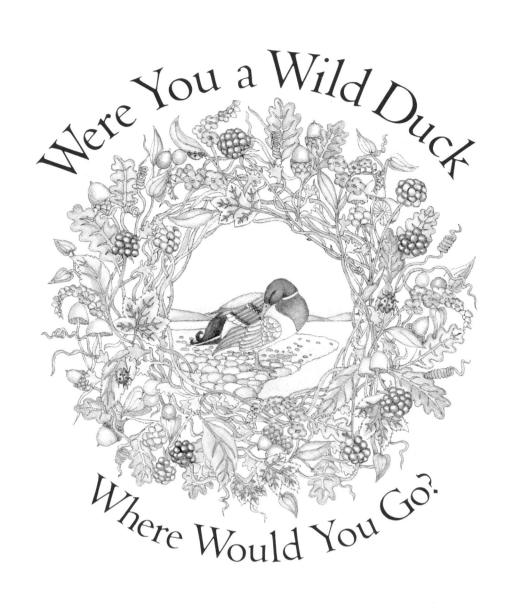

by George Mendoza

Illustrations by Jane Osborn–Smith

Stewart, Tabori & Chang
New York

Through endless time they follow their shadowless
tracks, and at the height of noon they hide in the
shade of their wings, as kings and prophets shield
their grieving hearts.

St.-John Perse

For my children, Ashley and Ryan, with hopes for a
better world . . .
—G.M.

For Peter and Theo
—J. O-S.

Text copyright © 1990 George Mendoza
Illustrations copyright © 1990 Jane Osborn-Smith

Designed by Paul Zakris

Published in 1990 by
Stewart, Tabori & Chang, Inc.
740 Broadway, New York, New York 10003

Library of Congress Cataloging-in-Publication Data
Mendoza, George.
    Were you a wild duck, where would you go? / by George Mendoza;
illustrations by Jane Osborn-Smith.
       p. cm.
    Summary: A wild duck narrator looks at the past when the
environment was bountiful, searches through today's polluted
environment for a home, and encourages saving and restoring the
environment for the future.
    ISBN 1-55670-136-5
    [1. Pollution—Fiction.   2. Environmental protection—Fiction.
3. Ducks—Fiction.   4. Stories in rhyme.]   I. Osborn-Smith, Jane,
ill. II. Title.
PZ8.3.M55164We   1990
[Fic]—dc20   89-28596
                                                                 CIP
                                                                  AC

Distributed in the U.S. by Workman Publishing,
708 Broadway, New York, New York 10003
Distributed in Canada by Canadian Manda Group,
P.O. Box 920 Station U, Toronto, Ontario M8Z 5P9
Distributed in all other territories by
Little, Brown and Company, International Division,
34 Beacon Street, Boston, Massachusetts 02108

Printed in Japan

10 9 8 7 6 5 4 3 2 1

Have you heard a bird call out
from the branches of a rookery?
Are not the songsters of the sky
like the spirit of the child?

Mallard is my name.

I am a wetland bird.

My duck-head glitters emerald-green;

chestnut plumes enfold me like a stately cloak,

my feathery fortress against earth and sky;

round my neck I wear a proud white ring.

If you saw me pairing out across

the prairies flowing you would see

the way I spring on wing

and hie over woods and ponds.

Whee-o-whee, as I go wheeling, scooping,
up-wind darting, earthward diving, loop-a-day,
gone is yesterday when the world was wild and free;
and all feathered sailors, wings curved against the sky,
could find sanctuary from the Mississippi flyway
and beyond to seas of far crimson sunsets.

Now what would you do
were you a wild duck,
a resplendent-feathered mallard,
or blue-winged teal,
your wings weary after your long flight,
and you found your land scorched
under the sun's cracking blaze,
furrowed like an old Indian chief's face?

And what would you do
were you a wild duck,
and the land where you nested
stretched barren without trees?
You circle, you look, you try to spy
your watering holes, your cattails,
your brushy ponds.
But they're not there.
Where have they gone?

Were you a wild duck
night-winging by candle of moon
from the salt-marshes of the Carolinas
to prairie potholes under northern skies,
and you suddenly found your glacial paradise gone,
where would you fly?

Where is the land?
Has it blown away?

I can recall once-upon-a-time
when the world was a bird's fairy tale,
a refuge for sea birds and desert birds
and woodland birds;
and when it came time for our nesting call,
all in abundance flew.
Then clouds took us in and clouds poured us out.

Safe and lovely, green and lush and deep—
this was our paradise.
Now, visions of long ago:
trout leaping in the tails of pools at evening time,
insects more than a bird could eat,
deer sipping by the pond's edge, downriver a moose.
A bear rears up, an owl hoots through thickening fog,
a fisherman appears along the river's mossy bank,
and wades soundlessly into the current pebbly with stars,
casting his line, silvery-liquid, under falling night.

I've seen this fisherman before with boots and creel,
hatbent over changing flies;
under astral light, bats and swallows play this fisherman
as a two-branch tree with a bug sailing back and forth
at the tip of his bough;
he is no scarecrow for birds in the twilight hour.

What frightens a wetland bird?
Greed. Mankind needing everything bigger,
with no thought of what
would make a better world.

Now I fly to find a friendly tree for shade,
but there is no leafy bough to rest upon,
no dappled, frog-filled ponds,
no musical wilderness shelters me.
And where are the calls of all my friends?
Where are the grouse, the woodcock,
the other birds I used to know?
Where are the mayflies that once emerged to dance
fluttering golden over ponds of blue light?
Where are the berries wild that used to grow
through prairie winds and song?
Where has my paradise gone?
Do you know?

You, my children, you will cry:
"Fly on, wild duck, don't despair!"
But who can tell me where?
I fly and fly yet reach strange places
unnatural for a mallard to be.

Were you a wild duck, what would you do?
Where, young witness, with wings-of-a-dreamer,
would you go?

Look up as I spring on wing
in search of woods and ponds;
I'll write you a cloud-poem, a child-song,
with wings lifting on currents of hope.

Where-o-whirring are the children
who will hoot with the owl through pine needles dark,
who will sing my song with me?

Let us save the marshes and the trees;
let us protect the prairies and love the land;
let us bless the rivers and the ponds;
let us guard the oceans so that great whales
might endlessly spume their journey songs.
For we are the children
who can soar above the greed of our day
so that a wild duck might fly, wild and free again,
forever-o-every day.

Lead the way
and we'll fly together
skimming meadows where it's always spring,
where rivers channel blue and silver-clear
with clouds upon clouds all mirrored there,
and wing to wing, under wing,
we'll watch the world glide by,
knowing we can find, at any time,
our wind-brushed bough.